First Flight

The Story of
Tom Tate and the Wright Brothers

story by George Shea
pictures by Don Bolognese

HarperCollins*Publishers*

To Grady Tate

—G. S.

Acknowledgments

The author would like to thank Tom Crouch, Chairman, Department of Aeronautics, National Air and Space Museum at the Smithsonian Institution in Washington, D.C., for his generous assistance. He would also like to extend his thanks to Tom Tate's son, Grady, and other members of the Tate family.

The artist and the editors would like to thank Elaine Raphael for her creative help in the painting of the illustrations.

First Flight
The Story of Tom Tate and the Wright Brothers
Text copyright © 1997 by George Shea
Illustrations copyright © 1997 by Don Bolognese
Printed in the U.S.A. All rights reserved.

Library of Congress Cataloging-in-Publication Data
Shea, George.
   First flight : the story of Tom Tate and the Wright brothers / story by George Shea ; pictures by Don Bolognese.
        p.   cm. — (An I can read chapter book)
   Summary: A boy named Tom Tate meets Orville and Wilbur Wright and witnesses the invention of the airplane in Kitty Hawk, North Carolina.
   ISBN 0-06-024503-4. — ISBN 0-06-024504-2 (lib. bdg.)
   1. Wright, Orville, 1871–1948—Juvenile literature.   2. Wright, Wilbur, 1867–1912—Juvenile literature.   3. Aeronautics—United States—Biography—Juvenile literature.   [1. Wright, Orville, 1871–1948.   2. Wright, Wilbur, 1867–1912.   3. Aeronautics—Biography.]   I. Bolognese, Don, ill.   II.Title.
TL540.W7S4   1997   95-17142
629.13'0092'2—dc20   CIP
[B]   AC

1   2   3   4   5   6   7   8   9   10
❖
First Edition

Contents

Chapter One

1900

Kitty Hawk, North Carolina

One morning, Tom Tate went out fishing. The first fish he caught was too little, so he threw it back. Then he caught a bigger fish.

"This could feed me and Pa for days," he said to himself.

Down the beach, Tom saw two men near a big tent. Tom walked over to see what they were doing.

"Hello," said one of the men. "That's a big fish you've got there."

"You should have seen the first one I caught!" said Tom. "It was as big as a whale. It was so big, I couldn't even pull it up on the beach."

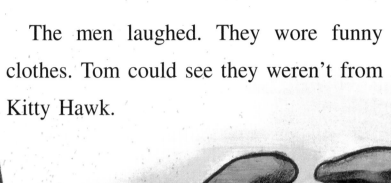

The men laughed. They wore funny
clothes. Tom could see they weren't from
Kitty Hawk.

"My name is Orville. Orville Wright," said one of the men. "You can call me Orv. This is my brother, Wilbur."

"Call me Will," said the other man.

"I'm Tom Tate," said Tom. "What are you doing here in Kitty Hawk?"

"We came here from Ohio to build a flying machine," said Will.

"What's that?" asked Tom.

"See for yourself," said Will. "This machine will fly through the air."

"What makes it fly?" Tom asked.

"The same thing that makes a kite fly— the wind," said Orv. "That's why we came to Kitty Hawk. This is one of the windiest places in America."

"The sand makes a soft place to land, too," added Will.

"Can I ride on it?" asked Tom.

"It's not finished yet," said Will, "but come back later and we will see."

"Okay," said Tom. "I will."

Tom was imagining himself flying through the air when he ran into his cousins Ned and Laura.

"I just met two men from Ohio," Tom said. "They say they are going to fly through the air like birds!"

"Oh, Tom," said Laura, "don't tell us more of your silly stories."

"It's true," said Tom. "They showed me a flying machine they've built."

"There aren't any such things as flying machines," said Ned. "You're making it up."

"Just wait," said Tom. "You'll see."

Ned and Laura laughed, but for once Tom knew he was telling the truth.

Chapter Two
The Next Day

Tom was on his way to see Will and Orv when he saw something big in the sky. It was the flying machine! He ran to the beach.

Will and Orv were flying the machine like a kite. Tom's pa and his uncle Bill were helping them.

When the machine came down, Tom asked, "Can you fly in it?"

"I have," said Will, "but just once. There isn't enough wind to lift me or Orv into the air today."

"I'm not heavy," said Tom. "Could I ride in it?"

Will turned to Tom's pa. "What do you say, Mr. Tate?"

"We won't let him go up too high," said Orv.

"Okay," said Pa. "But be careful!"

Tom stretched out on the lower wing.
Then Will and Tom's pa picked up the
machine and ran with it straight into the
wind. When the wind lifted the machine
up, they let it go.

Up, up it went! Tom was high over Kitty Hawk. He kept going higher and higher. Suddenly the machine began to shake up and down.

15

"Hang on, Tom!" Will shouted. Will and Uncle Bill pulled hard on the rope. The machine started to come down.

Tom shut his eyes as the machine skidded into the soft sand.

"Are you all right?" Pa asked.

Tom felt shaky as he stood up. "I'm okay," he said. "Let me go again. Next time I'll go even higher!"

"No," said Pa. "That's enough for today."

On his way home, Tom saw Ned and Laura. "I flew in the flying machine!" he said. "I was way up in the sky!"

"Stop making up stories," said Laura.

"My pa says flying machines are just foolishness," Ned said. "He says if people were meant to fly, they would be born with wings."

"You just come to the beach tomorrow," said Tom. "Maybe Will and Orv will give you a ride."

The next afternoon, Laura and Ned
came to the beach, but there was no wind.
The machine sat on the sand like a big
bug.

"When are you going to fly, Tom?"
Laura asked, and laughed.

"Look at me," said Ned. "I'm flying!"
He and Laura ran around laughing and
flapping their arms.

"Just wait," said Tom. "You'll see."

A couple of days later, Will flew again. He stayed in the air fifteen seconds and made glides as long as four hundred feet.

Then he and Orv began to pack up to go home to Ohio.

"Are you going away for good?" Tom asked.

"No," said Will. "This is a fine machine. It can go up and down and side to side. But we're going home to build a better one that will stay in the air longer."

"We'll be back next summer to try it out," said Orv.

"I'll be here to help," said Tom.

Chapter Three
1901

Will and Orv returned the next summer with a new machine. It was more than twice the size of the first one.

"This is the biggest glider ever built," said Will.

"The wings are longer and more curved than on our last machine," said Orv. "We think these wings will help us stay up longer."

Will flew first. He glided for a moment,

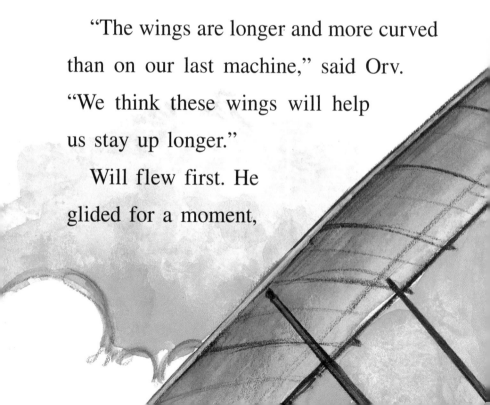

but suddenly the machine
spun around and
began to fall
very fast.

"Hang on, Will!" cried Orv.

The machine hit the ground hard.

"Are you all right?" Tom asked.

Will had a black eye and a bloody nose, but otherwise he was not badly hurt.

Will and Orv had to fix the machine, so they gave Tom's pa a job helping them. In a few days it could fly again, but something was still not right. At times it would stop suddenly and spin toward the ground.

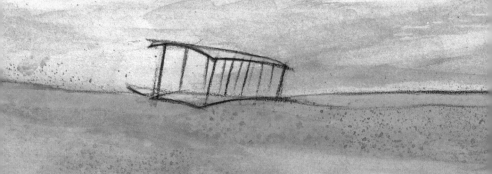

"What's wrong?" Tom asked.

"We don't know," said Orv.

"They may not know what's wrong," Pa said to Tom. "But I know I don't want you riding in that thing. It isn't safe."

Will and Orv kept trying different adjustments, but something was still wrong. Finally, they decided to return to Ohio.

"You're not giving up, are you?" asked Tom.

"I don't think men will fly for a thousand years," said Will.

Tom watched as Will and Orv walked away down the beach. He didn't think he would ever see them again.

Chapter Four

1902

That winter passed slowly. One day Tom got a letter from Orv.

"We have built a new machine with different wings," the letter began. "The wings are longer and more narrow. We have also added a tail for balance and to make better turns. We are coming back to Kitty Hawk to try it out."

Will and Orv returned in September. Once again they gave Tom's pa a job helping them.

The new machine worked much better than the last one. Will and Orv made almost a thousand glides in it.

"This is the machine we want," said Will. "We can control it. It will go up when we want it to go up. And it will go down when we want it to go down."

"And it will turn when you want it to turn," Tom said.

"There is still one thing this machine won't do," said Will. "It won't fly without the wind."

"We're going to put an engine on it," said Orv. "Then it will fly by itself, and we'll do something no one has ever done before. We'll really fly!"

That winter, in Ohio, Will and Orv built an engine and propellers to push the machine through the air.

But would it work? To find out, they would have to go back to Kitty Hawk.

Chapter Five
1903

Will and Orv brought the new machine to Kitty Hawk. Right away things started to go wrong with the propellers. Orv had to go back to Ohio to make new ones.

When he returned, storms with high winds made it dangerous to fly.

One day, after a terrible storm, Tom's pa said, "It's impossible to fly in this weather. If those two don't stop soon, someone is going to get hurt. I don't want it to be you, Tom. I want you to stay away from the camp."

"But Pa," said Tom, "Will and Orv are my friends."

"It's too dangerous," said Pa.

Tom missed Will and Orv, and he wondered about their machine. The weather was getting worse. What if they tried to fly?

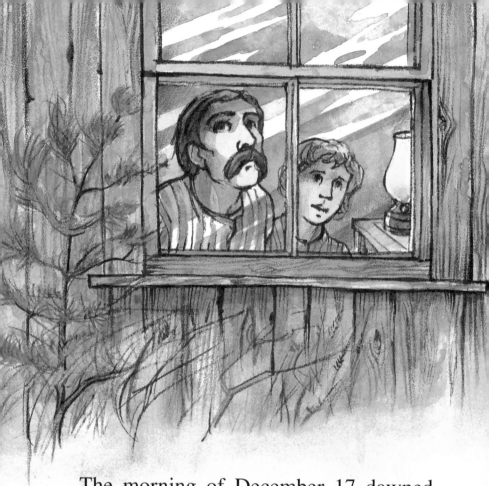

The morning of December 17 dawned very cold. The wind howled and shook the windows of Tom's house.

"They'd be crazy to try to fly in this wind," said Tom's pa. "I'm going back to bed."

While his pa slept, Tom left the house and headed down to the beach.

Tom saw a bunch of rescue workers from the nearby lifesaving station standing by Will and Orv's camp. It was the rescue workers' job to save sailors in storms. Had something happened to Will and Orv?

Then Tom spotted the brothers.

"We're going to try to fly today," said Orv. "These men have come to help us."

Tom helped the men pick up the machine and put it on a long wooden track. Everything was ready, but the wind still howled.

"This is it, Orv," said Will. The brothers looked at each other for a long time, as if they might never see one another again.

Then Orv climbed into the machine.

"Good luck, Orv!" Tom shouted.

Chapter Six
The Same Day

As Orv started up the engine, everyone held his breath.

The wind was getting worse and
Orv would take off right into it.

The machine started to roll down the track. First it moved slowly against the wind, too slowly.

Suddenly Tom heard Pa's voice.

"Tom! What are you doing here?"

"Pa, look!" Tom cried.

Just then the machine began to rise into the air. It jumped up and down in the wind like a crazy bird, but the machine was flying!

Everyone let out a big cheer, even Tom's pa.

"Well, how about that?" Pa said. "I never thought they would make it."

The machine flew for only twelve seconds and went only one hundred and

twenty feet, but that was enough. For the first time in history, a machine controlled by a human being flew under its own power.

Will and Orv made three more flights that morning. After the last one, everyone went into Kitty Hawk.

People shook Will's and Orv's hands and shouted, "They did it!"

Laura and Ned were there too. "Is it true, Tom?" they asked.

"Of course it's true," said Tom. "I told you Will and Orv would fly."

"We flew and Tom helped us," said Will.

"When will you fly again?" Laura asked.

"Will and I are going home for Christmas," said Orv, "but we'll be back."

"When they come back, they're going to let me fly the machine," said Tom. "I'll fly it all the way to the moon!"

"Will you ever stop making up stories, Tom?" asked Laura.

"No one will ever fly to the moon," Ned said, and laughed.

"Just wait," said Tom. "You'll see!"

Author's Note

Tom Tate was a real boy. He was born in Kitty Hawk, North Carolina, in 1888 and met Wilbur and Orville Wright when the brothers first came to Kitty Hawk in 1900.

They became friends, and Will and Orv really did send Tom up in their first "kite" flying machine. Following Will's first flight, Tom was the second person to fly in the Wrights' glider.

Tom's pa, Dan Tate, was employed by Will and Orv, and Tom's uncle, Bill Tate, also helped the Wright brothers.

Tom spent his whole life around Kitty Hawk, where he was a fisherman and a hunter. He flew in an airplane only one other time, in 1926. Tom died in 1956.

Tom never did fly to the moon. Nor did Will or Orv, but in 1969, when astronaut Neil Armstrong set foot on the moon, he honored the Wright brothers' work. He carried with him a piece of cloth from their first powered flight machine—the one that made that first brave flight the cold and windy morning of December 17, 1903.